A Note to Parents

Read to your child...

★ Reading aloud is one of the best ways to develop your child's love of reading. Read together at least 20 minutes each day.

★ Laughter is contagious! Read with feeling. Show your child that reading is fun.

★ Take time to answer questions your child may have about the story. Linger over pages that interest your child.

...and your child will read to you.

★ Follow cues from your child to know when he wants to join in the reading.

★ Support your young reader. Give him a word whenever he asks for it.

★ Praise your child as he progresses. Your encouraging words will build his confidence.

You can help your Level 1 reader.

★ Reading begins with knowing how a book works. Show your child the title and where the story begins.

★ Ask your child to find picture clues on each page. Talk about what is happening in the story.

★ Point to the words as you read so your child can make the connection between the print and the story.

★ Ask your child to point to words she knows.

★ Let your child supply the rhyming words.

Most of all, enjoy your reading time together!

**—Bernice Cullinan, Ph.D.,
Professor of Reading, New York University**

Fisher-Price and related trademarks and copyrights are used under
license from Fisher-Price, Inc., a subsidiary of Mattel, Inc.,
East Aurora, NY 14052 U.S.A.
©2003, 2000 Mattel, Inc.
All Rights Reserved. **MADE IN CHINA**.
Published by Reader's Digest Children's Books
Reader's Digest Road, Pleasantville, NY U.S.A. 10570-7000
Copyright © 2000 Reader's Digest Children's Publishing, Inc.
All rights reserved. Reader's Digest Children's Books is a trademark
and Reader's Digest and All-Star Readers are registered trademarks of
The Reader's Digest Association, Inc.
Conforms to ASTM F963 and EN 71
10 9

Library of Congress Cataloging-in-Publication Data

Gabriel, Nat.
    A day with May / by Nat Gabriel ; illustrated by Jerry Smath.
      p. cm. — (All-star readers. Level 1)
    Summary: A brother and sister play indoors and outdoors on a rainy day.
    ISBN 1-57584-384-6 (alk. paper)
    [1. Rain and rainfall Fiction. 2. Brothers and sisters Fiction.
3. Stories in rhyme.]   I. Smath, Jerry, ill. II. Title. III. Series.
PZ8.3.G98954Day 2000   [E]—dc21   99-34717

A Day with May

by Nat Gabriel
illustrated by Jerry Smath

1
All-Star Readers®
Reader's Digest Children's Books™
Pleasantville, New York • Montréal, Québec

Dad is busy.

I help watch May.

It's raining outside.

It's an inside day.

May makes a party
for the cat.

Then, she plays dress-up.

She makes me wear a hat.

I make a tent.

May makes a mess.

Dad says, "Shall we take her out?"

I say, "Yes!"

May jumps in a puddle.
"Watch out, Dad!"

May's all muddy.
May feels glad!

May comes in,
but she's upset.

She wants to stay out.
She wants to stay wet!

I have a plan.
Dad says, "Okay!"

May is happy.
I saved the day!

May is done.
She's nice and dry.

Then May needs a nap . . .

and so do I.

Color in the star next to each word you can read.

☆ a   ☆ glad   ☆ mess   ☆ shall

☆ all   ☆ happy   ☆ muddy   ☆ she

☆ an   ☆ hat   ☆ nap   ☆ so

☆ and   ☆ have   ☆ needs   ☆ stay

☆ busy   ☆ help   ☆ nice   ☆ take

☆ but   ☆ her   ☆ okay   ☆ tent

☆ cat   ☆ I   ☆ out   ☆ the

☆ comes   ☆ in   ☆ outside   ☆ then

☆ Dad   ☆ inside   ☆ party   ☆ to

☆ day   ☆ is   ☆ plan   ☆ upset

☆ do   ☆ it   ☆ plays   ☆ wants

☆ done   ☆ jumps   ☆ puddle   ☆ watch

☆ dress-up   ☆ make   ☆ raining   ☆ we

☆ dry   ☆ makes   ☆ saved   ☆ wear

☆ feels   ☆ May   ☆ say   ☆ wet

☆ for   ☆ me   ☆ says   ☆ yes